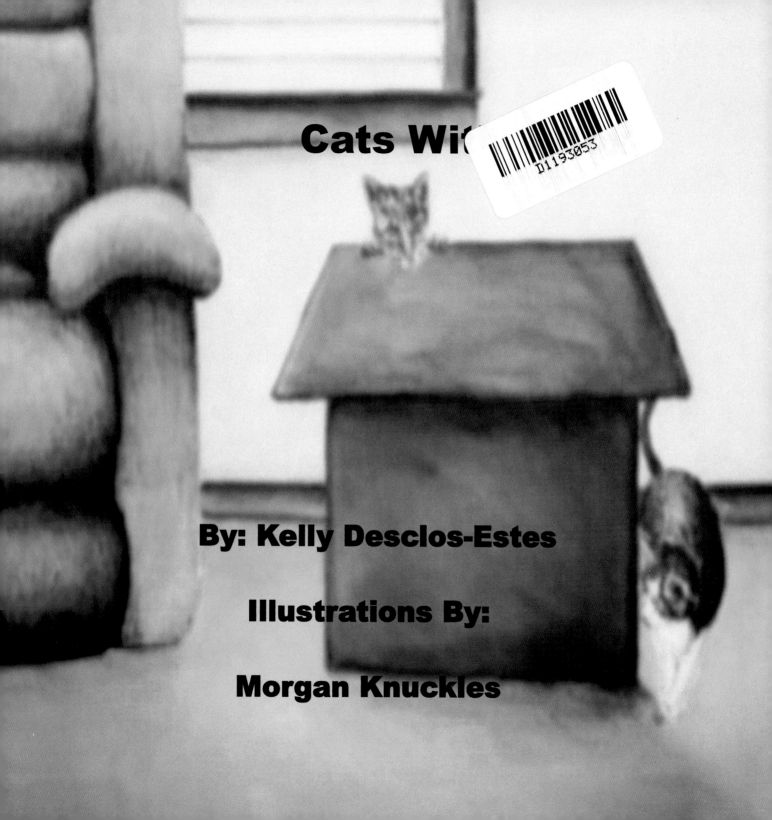

Cats Wit...

By: Kelly Desclos-Estes

Illustrations By:

Morgan Knuckles

ISBN-9780578618388
PUB 505-55

Acknowledgements:

I want to thank my husband, Shayne, for his love and support
through this process.

To my Social Media team, Writers' group, and dear friends Carol, Kate, Judy, and Laurie- I thank you for your encouragement. I especially want to thank Mary Moss and Andrea Perdue for their wisdom and expertise. Your "pushes" turned this idea into something real. To all involved in animal rescue and devoted to children in any way, thank you for all you do.

It is for <u>you</u> that this book is written.

I would be remised if I did not acknowledge the works of God in this endeavor. From the story's birth, my ability to expand my social media skills, to connecting with an illustrator-who happens to be the niece of one of my writers' group friends.

"We have gifts that differ according to the grace given to us" (Romans 12:6).

This book is dedicated to my son,
Richard (Richie) Estes, and his
rescue cat James.

James crossed the rainbow in 2018.
Richie left us unexpectedly in 2012.
Both lived 14 years.

A portion of the proceeds from the sale of this
book will be donated to an animal rescue
organization.

Cats With
a Box

When you leave out
an opened box,

A cat will
jump inside

Walking in a circle, he sniffs the corners and crinkles the brown paper.

He likes how
the paper
feels and
kneads it.

The cat stretches and kneads the paper until it is flat.

Then the cat lays down to take a nap.

**Suddenly, the cat
hears a noise**

**He slowly opens one eye
and sits up.**

Staying crouched in the box,
the cat waits for just

the right time.

In a flash, the cat springs
out from the box!

He jumps on the back of the other cat.
It's a surprise attack!

The two cats tumble and
wrestle on the floor.

They stare and
hiss at one another.

Then the cats chase
each other
across the room!

They go one way,
turn around, then
run the other way.

The cats make a sound
like galloping horses!

To take a rest, one cat
squirms behind the couch.

Thinking she has her play-mate trapped, the cat creeps closer to the couch from under the table.

With one pounce,
she has him!

He jumped
back
in the box.

He quietly walks in a circle.
He sniffs the corners and
crinkles the brown paper.

He slowly stretches and kneads the paper.

When the paper is flat the cat lays down...and takes a nap.

About the Author

Kelly is a graduate of Virginia Commonwealth University, and Master's level Counselor.
An experienced technical writer, Kelly is also a contributing writer to non-profits; currently working on a Bible Study. A life-long cat rescuer, Kelly enjoys shares stories about her "fur" babies.

About the Illustrator

Morgan Knuckles is a graduate of Missouri State University, with a Bachelors' degree in Art Education. She currently works as an Elementary Art Teacher in Orange County, California.
Morgan manages her own pet portrait business, Morgan Knuckle's Custom Artwork. She previously illustrated *We Are Our Dreams* by Judith Jerde. This is Morgan's first children's book illustration.

Contact Information

kdeewrites@gmail.com
Instagram: @kellydee_writes
Facebook:
kellydeewrites@kellydeeauthor
kellydees.com

mopaintspets@gmail.com
Instagram: @mopaintspets
Facebook: Morgan Knuckles Custom
Artwork

Made in the USA
Columbia, SC
21 February 2020